Say "Please!"

A Book About Manners

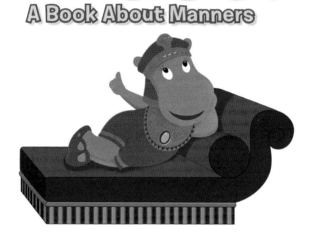

adapted by Catherine Lukas
based on the original teleplay by Janice Burgess
illustrated by Zina Saunders

SIMON AND SCHUSTER/NICKELODEON

Based on the TV series *Nick Jr. The Backyardigans*™ as seen on Nick Jr.

SIMON AND SCHUSTER
First published in Great Britain in 2007 by Simon & Schuster UK Ltd
Africa House, 64-78 Kingsway, London WC2B 6AH

Originally published in the USA in 2006 by Simon Spotlight,
an imprint of Simon & Schuster Children's Division, New York.

A CIP catalogue record for this book is available from the British Library

ISBN-10: 1847380298
ISBN-13: 9781847380296

Printed in China

10 9 8 7 6 5 4 3 2 1

Visit our websites: www.simonsays.co.uk
                    www.nickjr.co.uk

"It is I, Princess CleoTasha of ancient Egypt," said Tasha. "It's great to have a big palace and servants who wait on me. Hey! Where *are* my servants, anyway?"

Princess CleoTasha clapped her hands. "Servant Tyrone! Servant Pablo! Servant Austin! Time to wait on me!"

The three loyal royal servants hurried over to her. "I'm thirsty," she said. "Bring me a glass of water!"

"But there is no water, O Princess," said Pablo. "The River Nile has dried up."

"Well, fill it back up!" said the princess.

"Only you can, O Princess," said Austin. "You must ask Sphinx Uniqua to tell you the secret of the Nile. Only then will the water return."

"But first you must bring her three presents. They are hidden all over Egypt," said Tyrone.

"And we'll help you find them," said Austin.

Princess CleoTasha and her loyal servants set off to find
the presents.

"There's just one thing about Princess CleoTasha," said Pablo.

"She never says 'please,'" whispered Tyrone.

"Or 'thank you,'" mumbled Austin.

"What's the first present for the sphinx, Servant Tyrone?" asked Princess CleoTasha.

"It's called the Jewel of the Waters," answered Tyrone. "It is found inside the Hidden Pyramid."

They walked and walked and finally stopped in the Valley of the Pyramids. Then they noticed Servant Tyrone was leaning against something . . . something that they couldn't even see! It was the Hidden Pyramid! *Swish!* A door opened up.

Princess CleoTasha made Servant Tyrone go in first.
"Here it is, Princess," he said, pointing to a gleaming jewel.

"I found it!" the princess yelled, grabbing the huge jewel.
"The first present for the sphinx." She handed it to Tyrone. "It's heavy.
You carry it," she ordered him.

"She never says please," he murmured to himself.

"Okay, what's the second present, Servant Pablo?" asked the princess.

"It's the yellow lotus flower that grows on the Cliffs of Karnak," said Pablo.

"Let's get going," she ordered. "And don't forget my stuff."

The three loyal servants sighed. Once again she had forgotten to say "please" and "thank you."

After a long journey, they arrived at the Cliffs of Karnak.

"How am I supposed to get all the way up there?" asked the princess.

"The stairs, O Princess," Pablo explained.

"You go first," she ordered.

Servant Pablo shook his head. Once again she had not asked nicely.

Up, up, up they climbed. At the top of the cliff was a beautiful meadow filled with colourful lotus flowers.

Suddenly Servant Pablo spotted the only yellow flower and pointed to it.

"Oh! The yellow lotus flower! I found it!" the princess cried. She plucked the flower and handed it to Pablo. "You carry it. I have to walk down all those stairs."

"So do I," Pablo said quietly, as he followed her down the stairs.

"Behold, I found the second present for the sphinx!" announced the princess as she reached the bottom of the cliff. "Two presents down, one to go. Where to next?"

"To get the third present we must travel to the Secret Oasis," said Austin.

"Remind me, what's an oasis?" asked the princess.

"It's a green place with trees and water in the middle of the desert," Austin replied.

"Let's get that last present now," ordered the princess. "And don't forget my stuff."

The three loyal servants were all thinking the same thing: She forgot to say "please" again.

They all walked and walked until they reached the Secret Oasis.
"The third present is a drink of water from the Secret Oasis," said
Austin, handing the princess a golden cup.

"Great! I've got the third present!" the princess cheered. She scooped up the crystal-clear water and handed it to Servant Austin. "You carry it," she demanded. "Now that I have all three presents, it's time to go talk to that sphinx! Let's go, my loyal servants. To Sphinx Uniqua!"

They travelled through the desert along the dried-up banks of the Nile. At last they saw Sphinx Uniqua.

"Greetings, Sphinx Uniqua," said the princess. "I am the Royal Princess CleoTasha, and I have brought you three presents. They are the Jewel of the Waters, the yellow lotus flower, and a golden cup of water from the Secret Oasis."

"Thank you so much!" said Sphinx Uniqua. "What lovely presents! Did you get them all by yourself?"

"Of course not, O Sphinx," replied the princess. "My loyal servants helped me. And they carried all my stuff."

"I see. Did you say 'thank you' for all of their help?" Sphinx Uniqua asked.

"Well, no," said the princess. "But will you tell me the secret of the Nile so there will be water in Egypt again?"

"Okay," replied the sphinx.

"The secret to almost everything is to always say 'please' and 'thank you.' You can start by saying 'thank you' to your servants who did all the work for you," whispered Sphinx Uniqua to the princess.

The princess looked surprised. Then she turned to her servants.

"Thank you for helping me and for doing all of the work," she said nicely.

"You're welcome!" said all three of them together.

"And thank you, O Sphinx, for telling me the secret of the Nile," Princess CleoTasha said.

"You're welcome," said the Sphinx.

And just like that, the River Nile began filling back up with water.

Everyone cheered!

"And now won't you all *please* join me for a snack?" Tasha asked them
politely.

"Thank you! We'd love to!" said everyone else.

And they all went back to Tasha's house for a snack.